I0746759

2

Homecoming

ISBN: 978-1-956076-17-2

PROOFREADING and CREATIVE DIRECTION by NaBeela Washington
PROOFREADING by Keila Gallardo Cubas
LAYOUT and CREATIVE DIRECTION by Kristine Pham
COVER by Jordyn Flood

A Black journalist, photographer, poet, and art collector, NaBeela Washington holds a Master's in Creative Writing and English from Southern New Hampshire University and a Bachelor's in Visual Advertising from the University of Alabama at Birmingham. She is the Founder of Lucky Jefferson.

Keila Gallardo (she/he/they) is a freelance editor, translator, and sometimes writer. He was born in Peru but is based in Canada. She hopes to keep being an editor who can bring variety to the industry. They enjoy writing, watching shows, listening to music, and thinking too much about stories they like.

Kristine Pham is an Asian American illustrator and 2D animator with a BFA in Illustration and a Minor in Animation from the University of the Arts in Philadelphia. Kristine's work: kristinepham.art

Jordyn Flood is a designer and illustrator from Richmond, VA, who loves telling stories, creating characters, and is obsessed with mac and cheese! She currently works as a designer in the sports industry, but continues to do illustration in her free time, hoping to inspire the next generation of artists to share their own stories with the world.

Publication of Lucky Jefferson is made possible through community support.

Donate or submit to Lucky Jefferson on our website: luckyjefferson.com.

Foreword

"Home" is a loaded word.

For all the love and beauty it evokes, feelings of nostalgia, loss, and longing arise just as quickly. Many people are familiar with the specific disorientation of migration and displacement. Some of that memory is ancestral—our bodies recall the generations of before us who were forcibly removed from homelands and those who migrated across state lines and borders to escape oppression. For others, the realities of globalization and climate chaos have necessitated relocation to pursue economic opportunity of physical safety. Others have exited houses that felt more like domestic prisons than familial havens.

So few of us spend our lives in the same place. This is especially true for folks from the Black diaspora, navigating western cultures that weren't designed for us to thrive.

Still, Black folks seek to find, make, and protect "home." We cherish family recipe books and weave culture in our hair.

We commune with natural wonders that span from the Nigerian countryside to the Great Lakes. We treat our grannies like saints and, despite all odds, continue to reach for each other with love and generosity.

We seek to find home in our communities, in our culture, and in our bodies. In the Homecoming edition of Awake, it invites Black creatives to reflect lovingly on the spaces, places, and people that have made them feel at home like they are cherished and wanted. Whether it's a barber shop in their neighborhood, an auntie's kitchen table, or a favorite sweater. tenderness moves through each site of connection.

We unlock a kind of freedom and belonging that was forcibly taken from so many of our ancestors and us. We choose to orient toward community. Through each moment of creating home together, we guide each other back to ourselves.

Come join us.

Jasmine Barnes
Guest Editor

Melba Morel, *Home Is Where the Wind Doesn't Ask*

Amuri Morris, *Shelton Johnson Calls*

Lisa K. Bates, *You Have 17 New Notifications on the NextDoor App*

Gloria Ogo, *Where the Grease Pops Like Applause*

Khalisa Rae, *Ghetto. Ghet. Get. Begot.*

Asia Goins, *Dirt Don't Hurt*

Christian Hooper, *When I Tell My Coworkers Where I'm From*

Audley Puglisi, *boardwalk*

Mikayla Beaudrie, *Michigan Cherries*

Tamara J. Madison, *The Reach*

RESERVE
STO
ALL WA

Shelton Johnson Calls

— Amuri Morris

boardwork

— Audley Puglisi

I stand on the pier, staring out at the ocean. Faint outlines of boats dot the horizon: shipments, commerce. Behind me, the rumble of the roller coasters, a few screams as the cars click against the rickety wood. Some brave souls below the pier are swimming in the water.

Coney Island always stays the same.

Some Nuyorican old head blasts a Willie Colón joint, *pronto llegará el día de mi suerte.* An old man dressed in white sits beside the speakers, playing along on a *djembe.* A woman dances. She's her own drum, smashing her heels onto the boardwalk. Just behind me, I hear *nutcracker, nutcracker!* A thick Bajan accent soaring over the speakers, *sé que antes de mi murete.* I pass a woman with my grandmother's face. Is she on vacation? Two kids follow behind her. She opens her mouth and the South pours out. *Come on, now, keep up!* She says as the *djembe* grows, *seguro que mi suerte cambiará.*

Something unites us. Something hiding under all that pretty-pretty Spanish. I stare out at the Atlantic and it's almost too obvious. Of course, of course. And, for a brief second, I feel at home with complete strangers. A gaggle of New World misfits, trying to grasp for lost language. Stomping our feet onto the ground.

Dirt Don't Hurt

— Asia Goins

They say bread hits the ground crying.
So do I, some mornings.
And on this mid-February a.m.,
I've got my sides baked in blue.

Taxi rolled into Chefchaouen Monday.
Come Thursday, lost in a concrete sea:
Top crusted by Moroccan sun,
Flats funky from warm cobblestone.

First rest in days—
Dropping bread, bound to happen.
So I call my mother, anchored
thousands of miles west, where

Mama unpacks Daniel Fast groceries.
"What you eating out there?"
As she scrawls on a chicken-
shaped card: *We don't roosta like we usta!*

Serving teeth to an 80-something sista, hip
bruised from a Sunday fall. I recall
Mama's own fall. And her rise.
Blue steps behind her.

Mama's house phone hollers.
I tell her, "Take your time."
She chuckles. "I know, don't trip!"
They say bread hits the ground crying—

You can hear it.

Mama juggles her blood:
lines connect three of us, worlds
apart. Between calls and communion.
Our feet on the table.

"Tell that to your auntie—
you know she talking to herself now."
"Yeah, so what? I say hello when I come,
goodbye when I go. Like I always did."

Even after brittle flesh has gone bone,
you get used to sharing.
"Tell her what you eating in Morocco."
Salty things.

Lemon Tagine Chicken. Goat cheese, green
olives. Here, everything comes with bread.
And I heard bread hits the ground crying.
So do I, some mornings…

Travel feeds you funny.

So I pick it up. Dust it off. Kiss it.
Taste what's left.

Home Is Where the Wind Doesn't Ask

— Melba Morel

I didn't find home in a childhood bedroom
or passed-down recipes.
I found it in the ache of the ocean,
in the way salt clings to my skin
without asking me to explain myself.

There were years I didn't know where to belong.
Rooms filled with women cradling bellies,
appointments, prayers, questions with no return address—
and me, sitting with hands empty
but heart full of things I couldn't name.

Then came the sea.
Not with answers,
but with rhythm.

The wind never once asked what I could offer.
The tide never wondered why I came.
They made space for my grief
without needing it to be pretty.

Now, I wake early
and walk the stretch of shore that knows me best.
The sky, undone and quiet,
watches me lay down pieces of myself
like offerings: silence, breath,
the poem I carry in my spine.
This is my homecoming—
not to a person or place,
but to a self that no longer needs permission to exist.

I belong to this breeze,
to these waves,
to this unspoken peace
that rises from the sand and says,
You are whole.
Even now. Especially now.

Ghetto. Ghet. Get. Begot.

— Khalisa Thompson

for ICON (Shacondria) & Tank (Tarriona Ball)
for the girls with names too radiant to fold

Once
    in a group chat,
        a fellow Black poet
           got the nerve
               to call my name
                  "ghetto."
Said it
    like small talk.
 Like I wasn't supposed to feel
      the weapon—
         a needle prick
           laced in laughter,
             blood-wound
                ricocheting among poets
              who should
                 know better.
Too bad,
    this name be unshrinkable.
 A whole inheritance
    of baby oil
      and benediction.

A name born from
    altar cloth and afterbirth,
      wrapped in my grandmother's
        hush
          and
            hallelujah.

And I thought:
    how does a mouth
      trained in survival
        use *ghetto* like a slur?

Like we ain't already
    walking miracles
      names forged in fire,
        stretched like praise hands,
          hips wide with history,
            syllables thick and sweet
              as molasses.
I wept.
 Not just for me
    but for every girl
      who spelled her name
        before she could sing it.

For every
    pause at roll call.
 Every snicker.
    Every résumé turned ghost
      because a name
        carried too much
          Black.

That night, I called my homegirls
    the ones with names

adorned in oil-slick halos.

They said:
    Khalisa means
        pure.
            Sincere.
                Consecrated.

Our names
    be altars,
        passed down
            by prayer warriors,
                bathed in rosewater
                    and revival.
Still—
    that word *ghetto*
        rang in me like a church bell of shame.
 Like I swallowed it
    by accident,
        and it
            got lodged in my becoming.

Like I had to
    earn my right
        to be called.

He said *ghetto* like it meant
    cracked vinyl seats,
        Tupperware stained and warped,
            a roof stitched together
                with foil and hope.

And baby me
    believed that.
 Believed *ghetto* meant:
    rust,
        too much dreaming
            on the wrong block.

I came up in peak ghetto
    late '80s Gary, Indiana.
 Where sirens rocked you to sleep
    and lunch was bologna with mayo.

Where *ghetto* meant:
    potholes & crooked barbershop signs,
        bootlegs in trunks,
            struggle on display
                beneath a busted street light.

Some of us
    ate the word.
 Used it on each other
    like a dull blade—
        easier than bleeding alone.

But now?
    Now I know *ghetto* is:

        plastic still stuck on the good couch,
         collard juice slicking your elbow,
         chrome rims spinning like scripture,
         neon acrylics tapping testimony
            on the wheel.

Ghetto is:
    waiting hours
        for Lauryn Hill,
            because even if we ain't on time
                we arrive.

When we step in,
    all disco ball and afro-platform shoes
        we turn rooms
            to revival.

Ghetto is:
    fish plate sales from Cadillac windows,
      cousins lighting sage
        to cure hot comb burns,
      a living room turned Apollo
        and hair salon,
      a Kendrick beat drop
        that feels like deliverance.

Dictionaries can't carry us.
 Can't stretch wide enough to hold
    our cosmic nuisance,
    our rearview-cross holy ghost joy,
    our harmonies somewhere between
      Sexy Redd
        and the Isley Brothers.

We are:
    gospel and glint,
    cornbread and cosmos,
    a thousand textures
      braided bold.

So say it:
    ghetto.
 Say it gutter-holy.
 Say it like
    your tongue just saw God.

Let your throat catch glitter.
 Let it interrupt your peace,
a praise break
     at the board meeting.

Say:
    divine.

    chosen.
    queen.
    holy wrecking ball
      swinging through your bias.

I will not shrink.
    Will not soften my syllables
      to soothe your discomfort.

So if this crown is *ghetto*
    then let it be that.
      All day.
        Every day.

Ghetto. Ghet. Get. Begot.
 So freaking beautiful,
    you gon' need two hands
      and another language
        just to hold me.

Where the Grease Pops Like Applause

— Gloria Ogo

There's a place between 135th and don't-you-worry
where my auntie stirs truth into red beans,
and the kitchen sings like a gospel choir
on a Sunday with no hurry.

The table's legs are uneven,
but we balance it with old Ebony magazines—
the ones with Diana on the cover,
still fierce, still shining
through gravy stains and heat.

Here, home is the soft slap of dominoes,
the thump of bass from the back room,
the way my cousin shouts
who cut the spades like that?
and nobody answers
because the greens need tending
and the sweet tea needs more sugar
and the world is still outside,
but not here.
Not in this house.

Here, we pass stories down
with the hot sauce.
We call each other nicknames
long after we've outgrown them.
The screen door squeals when it closes,
and that's how you know you made it.

Made it back.
To yourself.
To laughter that knows your middle name.
To hands that braid your edges tight
and ask about your heart while doing it.

They say home is a building—
I say it's a hum,
a scent,
a rhythm in the rice pot.

It's where the grease pops like applause
for every version of you that's ever survived.

You Have 17 New Notifications on the NextDoor App

— Lisa K. Bates

The neighbors are cooking out
By noon the grill lid is clanging
Uncles debating fire and briquettes
and times and temps

Cars all down the block
Cause no one can walk here anymore
Everyone brought everyone
Trunks popped
I never knew there was a love like this before

One cousin brought his new girl and she stuck to herself
One cousin still not over Dame
One cousin is late with the chicken
Cuz better not try that again or—
And who's the cousin letting my good air out?

Fix a plate
And cha-cha real smooth
Hold a cold can to the back of that baby's neck,
ripping and running in this hot sun

The sky stays on till past ten almost
Deepening blue
Wisps of smoke float over the fences
Smell wood chips, ribs,
Henny clouds
Smell just around the corner, a little weed
—y'all know mama doesn't like to see that!

Later as I lay in my bed
Drift on a lovely day
Hear

Pop!-pop!-pop!

One startled baby cries a second
then shush
the kids are cheering

And I watch the sparks shower down
Glitter through the trees

when I Tell My Coworkers Where I'm From

— Christian Hooper

I like to glue them together a mosaic.
How I long to hear the firm, rhythmic nuzzle
of waves against the jagged rocks; the flock
of seagulls arguing over lunch; clamoring
of the fishermen - Is it a *yellow perch*?
No no, that's a walleye - offering us unused bait
to extend the river's generous blessings.
The hustle music from summer gazebo cookouts
gets carried down the current & it learns how to sing
driftin' on a memory like a hazy imprint
until our cultures meld into firm, colorful tiles.
If the Detroit River could sing, it would sound
a lot like my dad: it has way too many stories to tell.

Michigan Cherries

— Mikayla Beaudrie

Where dingy and dark root their way up brick like overgrown vines,
Thirty-two teeth offer greetings before sounds get a chance.

Imprints sink into the carpet where footsteps beg to be followed,
While wispy black curls dangle over shoulders like curtains.

The door lock's closing click leads to slack jawed mouths,
Spilling out menacing secrets divulged from diary entries.

Lust a Prima Vista lingers around to dance upon tongues,
Only to leave the tart taste of freshly picked Michigan cherries.

The Reach

— Tamara J. Madison

I have no words for

we have become

we— this reaching

to find one,
another returning

this thing

season in, season out,
lights off, lights on,
chosen words, caulked silences
in private, public especially

across multitudes and divides,
between time and forbidden zones,
always this reach

to us.

SUBMIT TO LUCKY JEFFERSON

Lucky Jefferson's mission is simple: we publish social change.
Our vision is to see books reimagined to center the modern reader.

We use art to bring about a different world tomorrow than the one we know today.

Since our founding in 2018 and our transition to a 501(c)(3) in 2021, we have mobilized writers and artists by providing new spaces and methods for publication and inviting them to actively reshape the arts landscape to reflect their voices, experiences, and visions for the future.

Learn more + consider submitting at: luckyjefferson.com

FOLLOW US

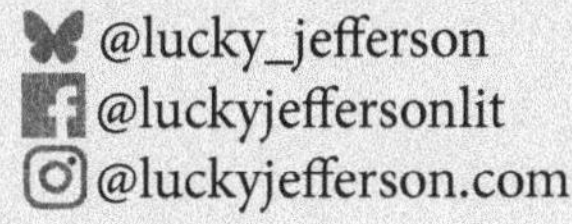

@lucky_jefferson
@luckyjeffersonlit
@luckyjefferson.com

STRIKE A POSE

Take a selfie with your copy of *Homecoming* and tag us!

HASHTAGSSSS

Use **#Homecoming**, or **#LJSQUAD** to follow the convo